GROLIER

Your partner in education

Distributed by Grolier, Sherman Turnpike
Danbury, Connecticut 06816

Grolier offers a varied selection of
children's book racks and tote bags.
For details on ordering, please write:
Grolier Direct Marketing
Sherman Turnpike
Danbury, CT 06816
Att: Premium Department

My Book

by Jane Belk Moncure
illustrated by Pam Peltier

THE CHILD'S WORLD
Mankato, MN 56001

Little  had a

She said, "I will fill my  box."

First I will find an umbrella.

I will run, run, run

to find an umbrella."

Why did Little  get under the box?

Why was the box upside down?

9

Little found an umbrella.

She found lots of umbrellas.

She put one umbrella over her head. Guess what she

did with the others?

Just then the sun came out.

Little put the put the umbrella down.

But then the rain came
down again.

Little put the
umbrella up.

Then she saw some underclothes.

They were getting wet.

She took the underclothes off the line.

She put them into her box.

Little  took the underclothes upstairs.

She put them away.

"Now I can play under my umbrella," she said.

She went out in the rain.

"I can run through a

mud puddle,"

she said. "What fun!"

Then Little u found an ugly duckling.

The ugly duckling was grumpy.

She put the ugly duckling

into her box.

"Do not be grumpy," she said.
"You will grow up to be beautiful."

Just then her uncle came by.

Little gave her uncle an umbrella.

Next, an umpire came by.

"Can you help us?" he said.

"We are playing baseball in the rain. We need umbrellas."

Little  said, "I have a box full of umbrellas."

She gave the umpire an umbrella.

Then she gave everyone

an umbrella.

ugly
duckling

underclothes

BOX

umbrella

uncle

umpire

What fun they had in the rain.

27

More words with Little u.

undershirt

Uncle Sam

usher

umbrella bird

umbrella tree

29